Rob Scotton

Splat the Cat

HarperCollins*Publishers*

Special thanks to Maria.

Splat the Cat

Copyright © 2008 by Rob Scotton

Printed in the U.S.A.

All rights reserved. No part of this book may be used or reproduced in any manner whatsoever without written permission except in the case of brief quotations embodied in critical articles and reviews. For information address HarperCollins Children's Books, a division of HarperCollins Publishers, 10 East 53rd Street, New York, NY 10022.

www.harpercollinschildrens.com

Library of Congress Cataloging-in-Publication Data is available.

ISBN 978-0-06-083154-7 (trade bdg.) — ISBN 978-0-06-083155-4 (lib. bdg.)

Typography by Neil Swaab

10 11 12 13 LPR 10 9 8 7

❖

First Edition

For Maggie and her very own Splat cats —Spatz and Strawberry.

—R.S.

Splat

It was early in the morning
and Splat was wide awake.
Today was his first day at Cat School,
and his tail wiggled wildly with worry.

If I hide from the day, maybe
it'll go away, he thought.

It didn't go away.

"Time to get up," said his mom.

"Time to get dressed," said his mom.

"I don't have any clean socks, Mom.
Maybe I should go to school tomorrow instead?" said Splat.

"You don't wear socks," said his mom.

"I'm having a bad hair day, Mom. Maybe I should go to school tomorrow instead?" said Splat.

His mom combed his hair. "Purr-fect!" she said.

"Don't forget your lunchbox," said his mom.

I'll need a friend today,
thought Splat.

And he dropped his pet mouse, Seymour, into his lunchbox.

"Time to go," said his mom.

"The front door won't let me out, Mom."

"The gate won't let go of my fingers, Mom."

"The lamppost won't get out of my way, Mom."

"MOM!"

"You can ride your bike if you like, Splat," said his mom.

So he did. But he didn't say a single word.

"Welcome to Cat School," said a big, round cat.
"I'm Mrs. Wimpydimple, your teacher."

Splat's mom gave him a hug.
"I'll be back soon," she said.
"You'll be fine."

"Everyone, this is Splat.
Let's welcome him
into our class," said
Mrs. Wimpydimple.

"Hi,

Splat!"

Mrs. Wimpydimple began. "Cats are amazing," she said.

"We're clever, cunning, and quick."

"Am I amazing too?" asked Splat.

"Yes, you too," said Mrs. Wimpydimple.

"Cats climb trees, drink milk, and chase mice," she continued.

"Why do we chase mice?" asked Splat.
"It's what we do," replied Mrs. Wimpydimple.

"Why?" asked Splat.
"Because."

"Why?"

"Why?"

"Why?"

"Why?"

Mrs. Wimpydimple sighed.
"Lunchtime!" she announced.

Splat opened his lunchbox.

"Mouse!"

The cats did what cats do.

Seymour hid behind a glass bottle,

and when the cats saw
his face through the glass,

they screamed and ran away.

Seymour did what
all mice want to do.

"Stop!" cried Splat.

"SPLAT!"

They didn't stop.

"Enough!" Mrs. Wimpydimple said, and it ended. "It's milk time."

"Hurray!"

But the door to the milk cupboard was stuck.
"No milk today," announced Mrs. Wimpydimple.

"AWWWW."

Splat whispered into Seymour's ear.
Seymour nodded and then . . .

A moment later,
the door swung open.

"Yum!"

Mrs. Wimpydimple wrote again on the chalkboard.

Cats don't chase mice

"Hurray!" cheered the class.

Soon it was home time.
Splat's mom returned and gave him a hug.

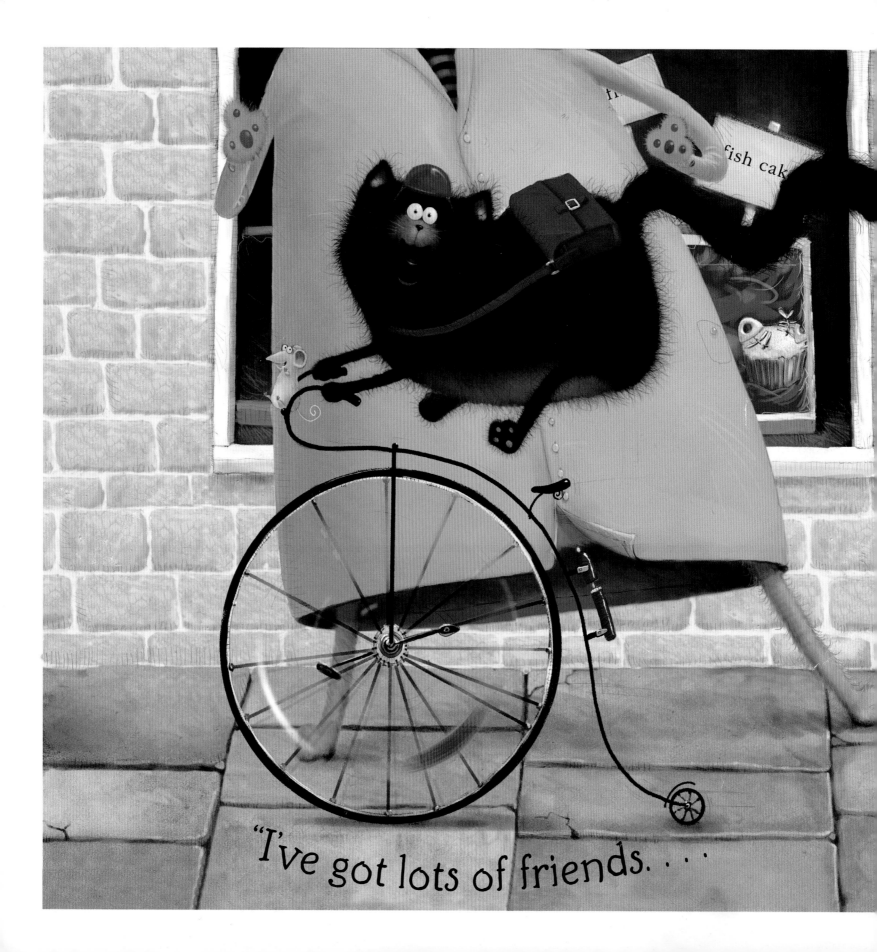

"I've got lots of friends. . . .

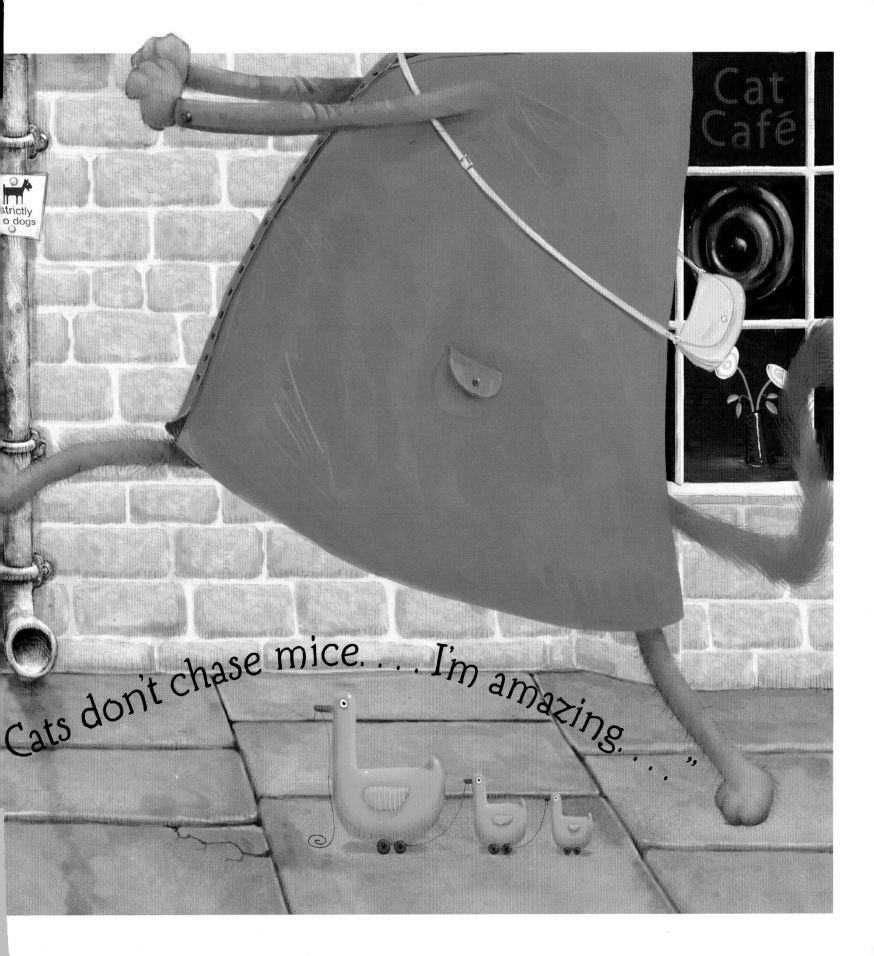

Cats don't chase mice. . . . I'm amazing. . . ."

It was early the next morning
and Splat was wide awake.
Today was his second day at Cat School,
and his tail wiggled wildly . . .

. . . with excitement.